DATE DUE

JUL 1 1 1984	AUG 1 2 2000	
AUG 2 1 1985	MAR 0 9 2003	
MAR 9 1985		
	FEB 2 6 2013	
SEP 2 3 1989	MAY 3 0 1990	
MAY 1 1986	JUL 8 1991	
NOV 1 3 1986		
MAR 1 9 1987	AUG 1 6 1992	
APR 1 0 1987		
AUG 2 4 1987	DEC 4 1991	
	DEC 1 4 1992	
OCT 1 3 1988		
	DEC 8 1993	
OCT 2 2 1988	JUN 1 2 1998	
APR 8 1989	DEC 1 0 '99	
SEP 2 6 1989	FEB 27 '01	
APR 2 0 1990	OCT 4 '01	
JUL 9 1990	JUN 2 '03	
	OCT 2 8 '04	

DEMCO 38-297

Go away,
Stay away

written and illustrated by **Gail E. Haley**

CHARLES SCRIBNER'S SONS   NEW YORK

1 3 5 7 9 11 13 15 17 19 RD/C 20 18 16 14 12 10 8 6 4 2
Library of Congress Cataloging in Publication Data
Haley, Gail E.
Go away, stay away
SUMMARY: The village people join in a festival to free themselves of the demons, goblins, and spirits that cause their misfortunes.
[1. Monsters — Fiction] I. Title.
PZ7.H1383Go   [E]   77-6759   ISBN O-684-15272-X

To the memory of George Einhart, my father.

With love and appreciation to Arnold, Marguerite and Geoffrey for their support and understanding when dinner was late. I am especially grateful to Mr. Schmid of the Swiss National Tourist Office, to the Horniman Museum, the Victoria and Albert Museum, the Museum of Mankind, the Royal Folklore Society and to the many folklorists, anthropologists and chroniclers who lovingly gathered and preserved the material which I have consulted.

All through the dark winter months the villagers stayed close to home. They were afraid of the spirits howling round their houses at night and scratching at the windowpanes. But when the warm air of spring finally came, it brought with it birdsong and flowers. It seemed as if the troublesome spirits had left with the ice and snow.

Then one day Mother's spinning wheel tipped over. The yarn unraveled and rolled across the floor. The wool lay entangled with dirt and ashes from the stove.

"How could I have been so stupid?" she wailed. "I've ruined my whole day's work."

Peter and his father heard the commotion and rushed indoors to see what had happened.

"There, there, Mother, don't fret," Father said. "I'm sure it wasn't your fault. The wheel was probably upset by the *Spinnikins*."

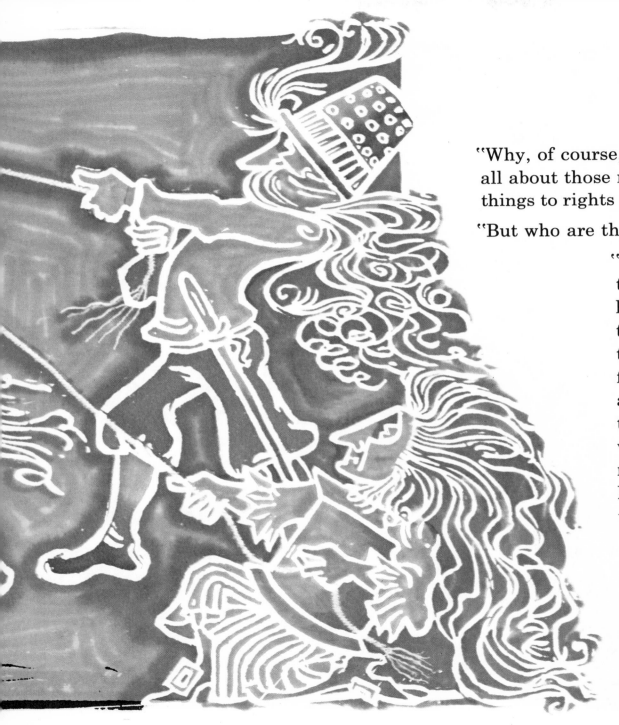

"Why, of course," said Mother. "I'd forgotten all about those nasty little *Spinnikins*. I'll set things to rights immediately."

"But who are the *Spinnikins*?" Peter asked.

"They are the imps who fly in through open windows and hide in the sewing basket. They tangle the thread, drop needles through cracks between the floor boards, blunt the scissors, and carry the thimbles off to their lair. And if the spinning wheel is left unattended for a moment while they are in the house, they'll pull it down and tangle the work."

Father went back to his carving. He was making a very special mask.

"What do *Spinnikins* look like?" Peter asked.

"I've never actually seen one," Father explained. "They only come out when no one's looking. But I've seen the mischief they cause."

"But if you can't see them, how do you know that they're really there?" Peter insisted. "Perhaps Mother turned the spinning wheel over herself?"

Father laughed. "You can usually tell the troubles caused by imps, goblins or spirits. For instance, that plate was full of hot sugar buns this morning. Now it's empty!"

"You must have eaten the whole plateful," his father teased. "I've been so busy carving, I haven't had a single one."

"I'm sure I couldn't have eaten them all," Peter said in a small voice.

"Well, the buns have certainly disappeared," Father mused, "Perhaps they were taken by the *Bunshee*—stolen from under our noses? Once the *Bunshee* starts eating something he likes, he can't stop until the plate is empty."

"He certainly was greedy," said Peter. "Do you think there are many other invisible creatures around?"

"I wouldn't be surprised," Father answered. "Winter spirits are always crotchety when spring comes, and most of the time they take it out on people."

In the valley far below, Peter's sister Maria sat in the sunlight, milking Queenie the cow. The sweet smell of clover filled the air. Bees droned sleepily in the blossoms. As the foaming milk streamed into the bucket, she dreamed of summer and of Carl the cowherd. Just at that moment she heard a shrill whistle, and there was Carl, beckoning to her from the cowshed.

"I've brought you the first flowers from the mountain," he said.

"Oh, they are beautiful!" Maria blushed. "They're just the color of the sky and sunshine. I don't think any day could be more perfect than this."

But when she returned to collect her milk, she found the pail lying on its side and the milk had soaked away into the ground. Tearfully, Maria trudged up the hill, carrying the empty pail.

"Oh, Father," Maria sobbed, "a whole pail of milk has been spilled, and I have no idea how it happened. I only turned my back for a second."

"Never mind, Maria," said her father. "I expect the pail was overturned by the *Kicklebucket*. He often lurks around the cowshed at this time of year."

"Do you really think it was the *Kicklebucket*?" Maria asked, drying her tears.

"I'm sure of it," Father said. "Now go and put Queenie into her stall before the *Kicklebucket* lures her off down the mountain."

Father had finished carving his mask, and now he began to paint it. Just then Peter's brother Ivan arrived, carrying in his arms fragments of an enormous cheese. The wooden cheese carrier, still strapped to his back, was empty.

"Father, I'm afraid I have bad news. I've had an accident with the cheese."

Ivan was crestfallen as he piled the broken pieces on the bench.

"It was hot climbing up to the cheese house," he explained, "and the sun made me drowsy. So, on the way down, I stopped to rest. Somehow I fell asleep and when I woke up, the cheese was lying at the bottom of the hill, smashed to pieces. I don't know how it could have got away from me; I'm sure I didn't sleep very long."

Father examined what was left of the cheese. "It looks like the work of the *Hobble Goblins*," he said. "They lie by the path, waiting for unwary travelers. Then they trip people up as they walk by. If anyone is unlucky enough to fall asleep, the little wretches rob him and scatter his belongings."

"I'm glad to know who really spoiled the cheese," Ivan sighed with relief. "I'll hurry to fetch another before it gets too dark. And this time no *Hobble Goblin* will catch *me* sleeping."

That evening Father brought out his finished mask to show the family.

"Everybody to bed early tonight. Tomorrow, before sunup, we'll join the procession to drive away the mischievous winter spirits that have been troubling us. You must put on your oldest clothes, and take with you anything that will make a lot of noise. Mother must shoo away the *Spinnikins*; Peter can get rid of the *Bunshee*; Maria can frighten off the *Kicklebucket*; Ivan must make sure that the *Hobble Goblins* trouble us no more. I will lead the whole procession."

Very early next morning, everyone in the village put on masks and ragged clothes, and joined the procession that wound in and out, up and down. They marched around every house, barn, and shed, ringing bells, shaking rattles, beating drums, and waving branches. As they marched they chanted:

"Go away; stay away!
Fiends and furies,
Ghosts and goblins;
Mean or menacing,
Cruel or careless.
Depart from our houses;
Fly from our village;
Return to your caves
And dark hiding places.
Go away; stay away!"

When all the demons were driven off, the villagers put away their old clothes and masks and their noise makers. Then they dressed in their best clothes to celebrate the arrival of a fresh, clean spring. They held a great feast and afterwards sang and danced all the rest of the day and far into the night. Even Peter was allowed to stay up late.

When we have accidents, break things carelessly, or hurt someone's feelings, we would rather blame an evil spirit than accept responsibility. Everyone feels that way now and then.

Festivals to drive away such evil spirits are still common in central European and Slavic countries. Carnivals, mummers' plays, and New Year resolutions are remnants of ancient exorcism.

This book tells of the kind of ritual that can still be found in season in Switzerland, Austria, Germany, Yugoslavia, Italy, and Greece. The Hobby Horse Dance that supposedly drove out demons, making way for a rebirth and for a joyous spring, is still performed in parts of England. These rituals are really forms of spring-cleaning of the soul.

Africans also celebrate this renewal with beautiful carved masks and costumes in the shape of animals and gods. In Indonesia, masks represent devils with frightening eyes and teeth. New Year is still the occasion in China when fearful dragons weave through the streets to drive whatever injures people into hiding. In the Pacific, among the Indians of North and South America, and in surviving Eskimo tribes, similar festivals in which masks are worn, rattles shaken, drums beaten, and bells and cymbals clashed, free people from the monsters that sometimes inhabit all of us.